Good Night Stories

Paul Fancett

AuthorHouse™ UK
1663 Liberty Drive
Bloomington, IN 47403 USA
www.authorhouse.co.uk
Phone: 0800 047 8203 (Domestic TFN)
+44 1908 723714 (International)

Because of the dynamic nature of the Internet, any web addresses or links contained in this book may have changed since publication and may no longer be valid. The views expressed in this work are solely those of the author and do not necessarily reflect the views of the publisher, and the publisher hereby disclaims any responsibility for them.

Any people depicted in stock imagery provided by Getty Images are models, and such images are being used for illustrative purposes only.
Certain stock imagery © Getty Images.

This book is printed on acid-free paper.

ISBN: 978-1-7283-9974-4 (sc)
ISBN: 978-1-7283-9973-7 (e)

Print information available on the last page.

Published by AuthorHouse 07/24/2020

authorHOUSE®

Good Night Stories

Billy the Bear

Billy was a bear who lived in woodland near a village, he was a well-known face to the villagers. At first they had been scared to have a bear living so close, but Billy had been living there since he was a young bear and they had come to accept him as part of the scenery. That is to say he had been there for so long no-one could remember a time when he had not been around, eating the apples from the trees that lined the road, or eating the blackberries from the hedges. As no-one could remember him ever causing any trouble, and the villagers had got used to him, it is true to say that a lot of them had become quite proud of their unofficial resident. According to some of the residents of the village Billy had been there for the best part of fifteen years now.

So it was that the village sign had been replaced with one which gave not only the name of the place, but also told people there were 657 residents living there and one bear. Most of the villagers called him Billy. The village was growing all the time and when a new estate was planned it was suggested the road should get called Billy Avenue, because it was destined to get built on the same path as Billy used when walking into the village from the wood. As an extra thank you for making the village a more interesting place to live, the Parish Council made the decision that the road should have a wide path on both sides of the road and no house on the end, so Billy could still come and go as he pleased. Also there should always be fruit trees planted in the green separating the path from the road. Although much of the fruit got eaten by the villagers, and the kids loved to climb the trees and used to knock a lot off, there were still lots of fruit left for Billy. Numerous folk used to come and watch him as he walked and grazed: strolling along and looking into people's gardens and windows.

It was about Easter time and the local television crew, which had been filming the village festivities, had some time to fill. They decided to fill it by filming Billy eating a few old windfalls and the way the villagers did not seem to mind him. In fact, several seemed to say hello as he passed. So it was hardly a surprise when they decided to end the news clip with a few shots of the bear at the festival. The clip actually finished by saying the large village festival was filled with big bunnies handing out chocolate eggs, also a bear eating apples (without their sticks) and that the bear won the apple-bobbing competition by bobbing six apples in under a minute, while in second place a resident only managed four.

This was the way fame came to the village. Every spring the community would throw a big party to celebrate spring and the following summer's crops. From what the locals said, if Billy turned up there would be a good harvest, if he did not then the harvest would be poor, but Billy always showed and the crops never failed.

The story most people liked best, though, is the one which tells it how it really was and is more about the time when the river was flowing well.

Some of the kids had built a raft and were sailing it down the river. If there had only been two kids on it the raft would have been perfect, but there were four and this made the raft unstable and liable to tip over. The other thing which did not help was that they were moving around a lot. With the first bit of rough water they hit, the raft tipped up and one of the kids went over the side. Unfortunately the child who went over was the youngest and had not yet learnt to swim. Now further downstream Billy was fishing for salmon, he saw the raft and the three boys trying to paddle frantically to the side and that was when Billy saw the fourth boy bobbing up and down in the water. Well, he was in the water already, so he took a couple of steps in the direction the boy was floating and as the boy went past, he poked his head under and plucked him from the water by his coat. He then carried him to the side, laid him down on the bank and nosed his tummy till he coughed the water out. Billy then lumbered downstream and soon overtook the raft. He jumped in and let the raft come against his shoulder and swam to the bank. As soon as the raft was still, the boys were off it and running back to their friend. When they arrived they found him alive and well, but cold and very wet. He was still scared as he could not remember what had happened. He thought he remembered Billy pulling him out and pushing his belly to get the water out but, "That *must* have been a dream, right?" he said to the other boys. "Well," they said "we saw him pluck you out and then we saw him nuzzle you before we disappeared around the corner. He definitely got us out, so it may have happened like that. It sounds right."

The boys started the long trek home and told their story to everyone they met. The whole village was amazed, but they were all in agreement. That very same evening the pub baked a big pie with corn, raisins, layered with apple and just to top it all off they put a sweet crumble on the top, sprinkling it with nutmeg. The following day the boys met up and took the pie back to the spot where Billy was still making the most of the good weather by fishing. When they got there Billy stopped and looked at the boys. They put the pie on the ground and backed away, the eldest starting to speak, telling Billy how the whole village loved him and thought this was a very good way to say thank you for saving the little lad.

"We wanted to say thank you, too, and we know something you will love." It was then the young boy brought out from the brush the biggest salmon that Billy had ever seen. The lad laid the salmon at Billy's feet and told Billy he was so happy to have a bear friend. "Thank you for saving me." For maybe one minute Billy stood still looking at the boys. He slowly walked forward, took a sniff of the pie and the fish, then looked up reaching forward with his nose and gently nudged the youngest lad's hand, then he nudged each other boy's hand in turn. He ate the pie, licking his lips and turning, so his side was to the boys. He lay down at the boys' feet and ate the fish. The youngest boy lay down next to Billy and gave him a big hug, soon the other boys were also hugging and stroking Billy from head to tail. So by the time Billy had finished his fish, he and the boys were good friends.

When the boys returned to the village the villagers asked how it had gone and the boys told everyone how Billy had loved the pie and the fish. They told people they thought Billy was lonely because he had shaken their hands, allowing them to cuddle up to him and that he seemed to like it. Lots of people agreed and said it was a shame he was alone, but if he was not then it would be very unlikely another bear would be as soft as Billy.

The village mayor was a nice old man and he heard what was being talked about. He went home and talked to his wife, then went and phoned an old friend who he had not spoken to for a while. A few days later some visitors came and talked to many people. They asked the boys to be their guides and take them to the woods. The boys said they would but they were curious. The visitors left and life returned to normal. Two weeks later they were back and this time they went straight to the boy's house, again asking them to come into the woods. This time the visitors drove and the boys sat up front. They were worried about the van but the men seemed nice and said, with a big smile "Do not worry, there is nothing to be worried about." *Could the boys trust them?*

When they reached the clearing the van stopped, the men got out, put a huge pie on the ground and climbed back in the van. It was then the youngest lad could not keep his worries in any longer and asked what was going on. The men said the mayor was a good friend and he had said they (the villagers) were worried about this bear. They were of the impression he was lonely. "It just so happens we run a programme which rescues bears. We have a bear who was brought up in captivity and have had her for a long time, because she needs some other soft bear to teach her how to live. In a nice place like this, where the locals will keep an eye on things and help, then she stands a good chance of being free. Now this is where we need your help. It would seem Billy trusts you, so it would be good if you could help with the introductions. What do you think? Are you up for it?" Before they could answer Billy was standing in front of them. The youngest boy jumped out of the van and quietly walked forward, moving the pie nearer to Billy. He walked up to Billy and stroked him, then gently led him towards the vehicle. They stopped when they could see into the back – there they saw the other bear. One of the men slowly got down, walked to the rear of the van, letting the back down. The boy looked at Billy and said, "She needs you to show her around and help her to fish." Billy nudged the boy's hand and licked his cheek, then walked to the pie. He picked it up and carried it to the van, looking at the other bear. She came down and the two of them tucked into the tasty pie.

Now the sign says 1525 people and four bears because Billy and Beryl have two cubs and all four come into the village and stop at the boy's house.

The moral of the story is: it is not what you know so much as who you know, and if you show friendship then you will get more friendship in return.

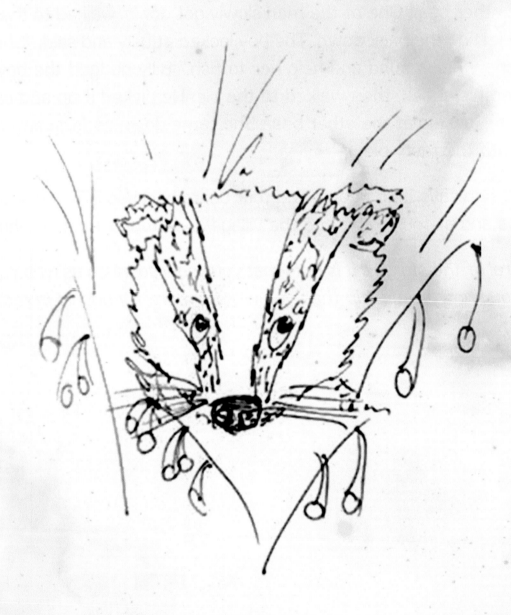

Brent the Badger

In a quiet, sunny little village one early morning the sun came up to find the cockerels rubbing sleep out of their eyes, and a little badger called Brent finding himself lost.

Now Brent, like lots of badgers, loves to eat bulbs and the previous evening, (evenings being the time when badgers become active,) he found a wood that was full of white flowering plants with big, broad, green leaves. In a distant memory he remembered his mum telling him these plants came from bulbs which were very smelly and very good to eat. If Brent were human then he might well have known these plants to be wild garlic. Brent had spent all night eating garlic bulbs and snuffling in the rich, dark earth under the trees, with his black and white striped face, eating his fill.

Maybe it was because he was still young, or maybe it was because he was full, he decided a little snooze would be fantastic. So he lay down and tucked his dirty nose in the bend of his back leg and drifted off into a nice, deep sleep. Sometime later he awoke having had a nice dream about slug-lined walkways, where he could amble along eating as he went. As you can imagine, he awoke wanting to eat some juicy slugs for dessert. He got up, wiping the end of his nose on the back of his arm, to try and get the bits of garlic out of his nostrils. He toddled off to look for some slugs. He was sure he had heard some of the old badgers talk of an old, dead, fallen tree down this way, and if this was true then there would definitely be slugs, mites and grubs under it. Brent ambled on down the path and to his surprise the wood came to an end, but the path did not. Well, what is a curious badger to do? Now, although Brent had never gone this far, he wanted to know what was ahead, so off he went. "The grass is short and wet so there might be

9

some slugs on the path, if I am really lucky," he thought, "then there might be some blackberries low enough to eat. Then again, it might be too early for them." So on he went, eating slugs as he walked and sucking up worms like spaghetti.

Having had a snooze Brent was not really sure what the time was. He knew he should be getting back to his sett under the big, old oak tree. Unfortunately this was going to be a bit more difficult than it would normally be, because he would ordinarily smell his way home. However all he could smell was the garlic which was still up his nose. Poor little Brent was totally lost. He had no idea which way he should be going and since the sun was poking its face over the sky-line, he could not go by the stars. Brent saw a mouse nearby, he went over and introduced himself by saying, "Hi, I am Brent the badger and I am lost. You wouldn't happen to have seen a wood around here, have you?" "Well," the mouse said, "hi yourself. I am Fred and I am a field mouse. What would I want with a wood?! So I am sorry, but no, I have not seen a wood. I have never been out of this field. Try asking Harold, he is a hedge sparrow and you will find him building his nest in the hedge by that hazel tree. He gets about a bit, he might have seen it." "Thank you," said Brent and off he went. When reaching the hazel tree he called out, "Harold, can you come down for a minute please?" Well, as he had been asked as nicely as that, Harold flew down straight away.

"What's up" chirped Harold, "you're out late aren't you? I thought badgers were supposed to be nocturnal creatures." Brent replied, "Ah, well, I am lost." "What! Badgers don't get lost. I thought you were supposed to have a good sense of smell. Whoever heard of a lost badger, how did that happen?"

"Well, you see, I spent most of the night eating garlic and some of the juice and bits got stuck up my nose. Now I can't smell anything, which is why am completely puzzled as to where I am. If I could find my way back to the wood then I would know where I am, but I do not know where the wood is nor how to find it."

Harold flew up high and circled around a bit before he came back. When he returned he settled in the tree on a low branch and told Brent he should follow the hedge in the direction he was pointing with his wing. Then he was to follow the hedge to the right through two fields, when it would lead to a big wood. Brent bid his new friends farewell and trundled off in the direction he was told to go. Sure enough, he did come up to a big bunch of trees but it did not seem right. These trees were different. They were tall and straight and the ground was springy underfoot. They were pine trees, not bent and twisted like his old oaks. Brent thought maybe this was just a bit of his wood he did not know. So he carried on regardless, hoping he would come upon something he recognised. The good news was that his sense of smell was coming back, but by now he was incredibly tired. So when he came to a tree whose roots were up in the air and the rest of the tree was on the ground, he pushed himself into the branches and tucking his nose under his paw, he fell asleep.

He did not know whether it was the soft ground, or the sweet aroma of the pine trees, but he slept really soundly and was woken up by a cold nose poking down his ear. He did not mind though, because the cold nose belonged to a lovely lady badger, who was an absolute stunner. "Hi, my name is Beth. Who are you?" "My name is Brent." Beth said she would show Brent around and share all the best places to eat with him. Brent soon forgot to ask if she knew where his wood was and stayed with Beth.

Dana the Duck

Dana was an ordinary duck living on an old, ordinary farm pond, eating ordinary food on ordinary days. So you would expect her life to be ordinary and boring, but Dana's life was anything but ordinary. Now whether it was due to an ancient yew tree or whether it was the hedge which was made from really old, twisted hawthorn, both of which are said to have magical powers, no-one was quite sure, but Dana's life was something that even people with the most vivid of imaginations could never have dreamt up. Now hold onto your hats because this story, no matter how hard to believe, could never have been dreamt up. It happened. "How do I know?" I hear you ask. Well, I know because I, Martha the mouse, was there. I bore witness to it.

It all started on one winter's morning when Dana came out of the duck-house a bit too quickly, by that I mean she was not yet fully awake. She tripped over the top of the ramp which leads from the duck-house to the pond and slid down the ramp on her ample behind, did a perfect somersault, only to land not on water but ice as the pond had frozen that night. Now Dana had never seen ice before and was not sure what to do. There she sat, freezing her rear-end but trying to collect her thoughts, composure and dignity. Well, if you know anything about ducks then you will realise this is a daft thing to try and do, as they don't have much of any of them to start with! Having done her best, Dana decided to look around to make sure no-one had seen it, then she tried to stand up. Well, she managed it, while looking beneath her and trying to work out how she was standing on the water. It was at this point she made her second mistake of the day, pecking the ice and going head over tail feathers again. This made me stop my munching and crunching on the last rose-hip of the season, as I was laughing too much to hold on.

Give Dana her due, in no time at all she was moving around the ice like a professional. Later, when it was about lunchtime, the farmer brought down the day's bread as usual. He came down the field in his big, noisy, smelly tractor and as normal he did not stop, he just opened the door and threw a handful of slices out of the door onto the pond. Normally this would have given way to a rush to see who would get to it first. Would it be Dana or Cindy the carp?

Today, obviously, Cindy stood no chance but Dana still made a dash for it and (as you might guess) this rush made Dana's foot start to spin, she ended up flat on her back on the ice, with the tip of her bill touching the biggest bit of bread, but what she saw made her roll over laughing. Cindy had also gone for the biggest bit and had come up to the bread, mouth open to suck the bread in, only to get her big lips stuck to the underside of the ice!

So as you can see, this was anything but an ordinary day. There is more to tell. When Dana had eaten all the bread, she waddled to the bank and sat preening her feathers, which was part of her normal routine. Today though, her feathers started to come out in clumps. Underneath the boring, old, white feathers were ones which were lovely colours, they were blue, brown, red, silver, pinks and the loveliest green I have ever seen. By the time she had finished Dana was sat in a comfy nest of downy feathers. She got up and waddled down to the pond to look at her reflection in the water only to find that the ice does not reflect like water. "Oh bother, fudge and catfish, I wish the water was liquid again, not solid," she said and into the water she went with a splash, but not before she caught sight of her bottom. "Wow," she thought "my bum does not look so big in this colour."

Well, the sudden disappearance of the solid water she thought a bit odd, but it had not been there the night before, so she was unaware that ice does not just disappear like that. The rest of the day passed uneventfully until she went to bed. As she went up the ramp, she remembered the nest of feathers and thought it would be nice to have that in the duck-house for a bed. Imagine her surprise when she went up in through the door and saw in her favourite corner the pile of feathers all soft and white and so warm.

She did not really start to wonder about events being odd, until she heard the tractor coming the following day, then she remembered the water being solid and how *she* had all the bread because Cindy could not reach it. Then she did a SILLY thing. Dana wished the water was solid again. "Why is that so silly?" I hear you ask. Well, think about it – where was Dana? She was in the water too, and now it was Cindy's turn to laugh as all Dana could do was quack and flap her wings, because she was frozen into the lake. Just to make things worse Cindy kept flapping Dana's feet with her tail. To add insult to injury, the bread the farmer threw landed all around Dana but none landed within reach. She struggled for quite some time trying to reach the bread then gave up and fell to thinking about the last couple of days and how lots of the things that she wanted had happened: like the coloured feathers, the nice, warm, comfy bed and then the way the water went solid this morning. "Oh!" she declared out loud, "If I could only turn back time I would not wish for it to happen."

With that the bread vanished as did the ice, and she realised she could hear the tractor coming through the field, and that maybe, just maybe, she could get what she wanted. That is where this story ends (or just about) because the farmer threw the bread into the pond, in his usual way, and as the bread soared over Dana's head she wished she could jump like the grasshoppers. *O n l y* - she did not think it through very well, as grasshoppers can't swim. In the blink of an eye, she was in the water and before she could wish herself out of it, Cindy gobbled her up.

So as you can guess, the moral of this story is quite obvious. Be careful for what you wish because you might get it.

Night, night, sweet dreams!

The end.

Eloise the Elephant

Eloise the elephant lived in Africa and as she was an African elephant she had the largest ears of the two types of elephant. In the animal kingdom the elephant is said to have the biggest brain and it is thought that elephants never forget. In Eloise's case this was true for she had a dream, one which never left her mind. She thought about this dream all the time. Her parents thought she was mad because of it, but it did not stop her dreaming.

Every summer the animals used to gather at the largest water-hole and have competitions, similar to our Olympics. They would have races, lift and jump, just to see who was the best at which event. It was usually only the males who took part but Eloise wanted to win, too. The elephants normally only did the lifting and the pushing, but Eloise wanted to do something different from the rest of them. She wanted to win the jumping, in particular the long-jumping! Now, as you know, elephants are big, heavy animals and are just not the right shape to jump, but Eloise had been told all the way through life "Do not ever give up," so she kept practicing. She would run towards the water-hole and try to jump off the bank but she ended up doing a nosedive down the slope into the water and making a big wave go across the water-hole. All the other animals used to laugh and make jokes about the mad elephant. It never stopped Eloise. She just kept on trying.

As everyone agreed that Eloise was mad she had very few friends. One animal who was a friend was George, he was one of the gazelles. The jumping was nearly always won by the gazelles. George asked Eloise one day "Why do you always keep charging the water?" "I am not charging the water," she replied indignantly. "I am trying to learn how to jump." Once

George had stopped laughing he said "If you are serious then I will try to help. It will need a lot of hard work on your behalf, but I am prepared to give it a go. However, you will *not* be ready for this year's event."

Each day after their morning's drink they slipped off into the bush, practiced and exercised. To start with George only got Eloise to get her front feet off the floor, then only to get her back feet off the floor. After a lot of practice, George told Eloise to get her back feet to come off the ground as her front feet were coming down, which in fact gave Eloise a hop. Next George got Eloise to run and do the hop. When she landed some of the trees around her lost some of their fruit, which she promptly ate. When they came out from the bush the other animals asked if they had felt the earth move and then wondered why they were both laughing so loudly! After that first time they quite often made the earth move and slowly Eloise managed more of a hop.

The day Eloise managed to get a hop as long as her body, was the day she really thought she *might* stand a chance at the competitions. The problem was that spring had already gone and the competitions were fast approaching. Eloise wanted to win *so* badly, not only for herself but to show everyone else she was *not* mad. George had got an idea some time ago, but Eloise was reluctant to consider it. "How do you know it will not work if you do not listen and give it a go?" he asked. "I will feel daft and look stupid," she complained. "You are right," said George, "but everyone is going to laugh at the thought of an elephant doing the long-jump anyway, and if I am right, this new technique will give you at least twice the distance you have now."

"OK. So what is this new and wonderful idea of yours anyway?" "Do you trust me?" asked George. "Well, you have got me this far haven't you, so I have no choice." George explained what he wanted Eloise to do, she was amazed. "You said you have to be stream-lined to get any distance, this is the complete opposite, it will never work." "Please try it and see," pleaded George. So Eloise took a run up to the starting mark they always used, she jumped and saw the previous landing mark sail beneath her as she soared twice the distance of her previous best. When she landed it was a gentle touchdown, she looked back and saw George grinning like Henry the hyena. "You are ready," George said.

A few days later the competitions started and as always the cheetahs won the running, the crocodiles won the swimming, Eloise's dad won the lifting and pulling and the zebras won the relay race. The last event of the day was the long-jump and as the gazelles lined up, Geraldine the giraffe announced they were to line up one at a time. As the line moved slowly forward, Eloise (who had taken up the last place in the line), came into view. Geraldine started to laugh. The line stopped and the crowd hushed until Geraldine composed herself and announced there was a surprise entry. Eloise was going to try the long-jump! The crowd laughed so loudly that it almost drowned out Eloise's charge. As Eloise hit the mark she did her biggest ever hop and opening her ears wide she jumped her longest ever jump – almost four times her own length: which although was not long enough to win, was long enough to beat some of the gazelles. This in turn hushed the onlookers, who then started to cheer and stomp the ground. From then on nobody thought Eloise was mad, in fact quite the opposite was true: they all congratulated her and said they did not know that elephants could jump. That was how Eloise became known as the 'not mad elephant'.

The end.

Franco the Frog

Franco the frog lived at the bottom of the garden, where the children of the house never played and the pets were not allowed. It was an overgrown area with a wind-fallen branch from the apple tree and all the summer grass cuttings were dumped against the hedge. These helped to keep the ground moist and warm which were the exact conditions Franco loved, partly because they were the conditions small creatures like worms, little flies, bugs and slugs liked as well, and Franco did enjoy eating them! Of course the rotting apples helped to attract the creatures as well, so more food for Franco to eat.

Franco was old for a frog: that is to say he was four winters old and he had seen many changes in the garden. The boggy ground had given way to a pond which lasted all winter and did not freeze, so all in all he had quite the easy life. He spent his days lazing in the sun with one eye open and the other inspecting the back of his eyelid, after a while they would swap. At night you could hear him croak to see if any of his neighbours were coming over to dinner, for Franco was known in gardens around for his parties. On this particular night he could hear a voice of a lady frog who he had not heard before, but the thing concerning him most was that the voice came from the 'dangerous garden', so called because it was across a busy road. So for frogs it was out of bounds. To make it even worse the garden was so overgrown that mice and rats lived there. As any frog knows, when you have mice you have cats, which can be really bad news to frogs. The rats would hurt a frog too.

Well, Franco tried to warn the new voice of this but the owner just carried on croaking, singing in its high pitched voice. This got Franco very curious and that is something Franco very rarely got, because frogs which get curious tend to get careless as well which tended to do them in. As Franco lived next to the road he knew how to handle traffic, seeing as how he had watched lots of cars and last spring he had some lessons from a field mouse. Although he was not overly interested, he had listened to what the mouse had said. He let his mind wander back to the spring before, when as usual he was sat with one eye open the other shut, he saw a mouse out of the corner of his eye run out onto the road. Half way across it stopped, sat down, and let the car pass right over the top of it before it continued across the road and into his garden. Now over the next few months Franco saw the mouse do this a lot and Mary (the mouse) and he became quite good friends.

Mary had decided to leave home because there were too many cats in the garden across the road, so she asked if Franco would mind if she took up residence in a nest under the branch. Mary, being a field mouse, lived on seeds and berries so Franco had no objections. Every night Mary would go across the road and eat her fill of the seeds and fruit growing in the wild, untamed garden, then return to her nest. It was then they would talk for a while. It was during one of these chats that Franco asked Mary about the road and why she would let the cars pass over her.

"What you do when you hear a car coming is you sit and wait. You will never outrun a car, but you can be clever and outsmart it. As the car comes around the corner you hold out both paws, cover the lights and keep them covered. If you have to move a bit then do so. As long as you are looking at the car and covering the lights, the car will go right over your head, then and only if there are no more cars, can you carry on your way."

Franco always remembered this because it was not long after this that Mary found a car which did not play the game. Franco was sat catching fruit flies for his dessert, when he saw Mary come onto the road and sit and wait as the car came around the corner. Franco was sure it should have had only the one light because it sounded like a bike, not a car. But two lights it did have. Mary gave Franco a quick wave and put her arms up. When the car had gone by, Franco saw that Mary would not be coming any more, as Mary had found out some cars have only three wheels. So what Franco did on the rare times he crossed the road was to wait until the last moment and then take two hops in the direction he was headed. This little modification had saved Franco now on three occasions, as the middle wheel whistled harmlessly past him.

So as Franco was curious about this other voice he had heard croaking, he thought he would go and pay a visit. He snapped up one more slug to see him on his way and set off across the road. He made it unmolested and started to hop over and through the vegetation, stopping only to answer the croaks and once to say hello to Mary's cousins, who were living under a rotting stump. He stopped suddenly and took a quick jump backwards as he could not believe his eyes. Where once there was wasteland was now a lovely garden with pretty flowers around the edges and short grass. There was a huge pond with a tree in it, creating an island. Sat on this island was the unknown frog croaking away. "Well, of all the strange things!" thought Franco.

"Stop! Stay there!" the frog croaked. Franco did not need to be told as he, too, had seen the cat heading across the garden, right towards the undergrowth in which he was hiding. Now that the cat had reached the undergrowth, it turned, put its back to Franco and started to stalk slowly through the long grass, obviously trying to catch a mouse. "That was lucky!" thought Franco. When the cat was far enough away, Franco started to hop for the pond and with one last big jump he went plop down into the deepest and clearest water he had ever known. Whilst he was exploring the water, he realised he was not alone. There were fish: gold ones, black and white ones plus all sorts of bugs. He was watching all this in wonderment when he was dapped on top of his head. He turned around to tell off this thing which had dapped him on the head only to be mesmerized. There before him was the prettiest frog he had ever seen. "Wow!" thought Franco. "Now there is a lady to have frog-spawn with."

All of a sudden a car horn blasted into the night and Franco realised he was in his own garden. It must have been a dream and he had not met a lovely lady frog. The garden next door was not like paradise .... or was it?

Franco took in an enormous breath and let out the biggest and loudest croak he had ever done, the night went quiet just for a second then he heard the first of several replies, which did come from the other side of the road. "Oh, can it be?" wondered Franco, so he repeated his croak and there it was again. Well, there was only one way to find out if the frog across the road was his dream frog. Franco sucked up one last slug to see him across the road and set off in search of his lady love. He crossed the path, hopped across the road and, as in the dream, no cars came. Then he hopped through the hole in the fence, past Mary's cousins, saying "Hi" as he went. He started to slow down as he remembered the wild part ending soon. True enough, the end was there as was the cat, but the cat was a long way away. As he crossed the garden he was amazed at how lovely it all was. He carried on into the pond with a big jump.

IT WAS TRUE! There in the pond was a beautiful lady frog called Floreanne. She took Franco's breath away. The feeling was mutual. They had a special cuddle and left a load of spawn in their wake. They both climbed up the bank of the island and shared their first kiss. Then they bid each other a good kip. Quite some time later, Franco awoke to find he was no longer lying next to Floreanne, but there was a human lady next to him. He was about to hop away, when he noticed with surprise that the lady might be as big as the island, but the island no longer looked big, quite the opposite. It looked small. The lady also did not look as big as she should?! He peered into the water and saw his own reflection, only to realise he had changed into a man! He bent over to give Floreanne a good morning kiss and tell her about the surprise awaiting her.

!HOW WOULD YOU EXPLAIN THAT TO THE PEOPLE WHO OWN THE GARDEN??????

The end.

Haden the Hare

Haden was a hare who lived at the top of an orchard and, unusually, his form was under an overgrown shed which had long since been forgotten by the humans and gave lovely cover. The thing Haden loved most about where he lived was that the grass under the trees was kept short. This was good for two reasons: one was that if it was short then Haden could see anything which might be a threat before it got too close, the other was that if the grass is short it always has new shoots and they are the most nutritious bits of grass a rabbit or hare can eat. Therefore Haden was a fit and healthy hare. As I am sure you know, the way to tell the difference between a rabbit and a hare is that a hare has a lot longer back legs, the ears are slightly longer and the very tips are black. The other reason Haden was lucky to have the best grass was because he was the champion boxer.

Every Friday night the local wildlife would come together and watch Haden fight, most of them would place a bet. The ring where the fights took place was set up in the shed above Haden's form. It was a good place because the smaller animals sat ring-side with the larger ones behind and the squirrels and birds would sit up in the eaves on the rafters.

As I said, the animals and birds would all wager money on who would win. Sorry, did I hear you ask how they can have money? Well, just because they are animals they *do* have money, how else would they buy the things they need, like clothes, soap and such-like? Now, of course, it was not metal and paper like the money we use. They used woodland money. They had acorn cups and leaves, which were good in summer and autumn, but really bad in winter and sometimes they used pretty stones too. This is probably the real reason animals hibernate, as without money they can't buy the things they need, making hibernation a necessity. So these boxing matches had two important uses: one was to keep everyone in touch; the other was to share the money around. The best thing was that the squirrels always lost, but as their drays (where the squirrels lived) were made of leaves, they were like the woodland bank, because as leaves dry they change colour. As with us, pink paper money is worth more than green, and squirrels know this, so during the winter their money grows in value.

Haden lived a lonely life except when he was in the ring, as he had no partner. This was the one thing he wanted most. He would sit up for hours reliving, not the fight, but the little bits of conversations which he had heard before, during and after the fight, wishing the crowds really wanted to talk to *him*.

Haden's one and only friend was Verity the bank vole, but she did not talk a lot and when she did, because she was small and did not go far, she did not know a lot. So talk with Verity was okay, but it was not exactly stimulating. However, to Haden it was definitely better than nothing.

One morning after a big storm had blown through the valley, Haden went out on his normal training run. He found the storm had blown over a big pine tree and left it blocking his path, so he headed downhill to go around it, but he ran into trouble. As normal Haden was running too fast; so because of his long back legs and shorter front ones, as the hill got steeper his little front legs could not keep up with his bigger, stronger back legs and it was not long before he was rolling head over tail down the hill, only to land in the stream at the bottom with a splash. Whilst he sat there cursing himself for being a fool, he became aware of some gentle laughter and this he did not like! As he turned around he saw it was another hare like himself.

"OK and what is so funny?" he asked. "Well, if you had seen yourself rolling down the hill and ending up in the drink, you would have seen the funny side too, especially after the last few hours I have had. You see, the wind last night ripped out the tree my home was under and now I have not got a home, so thank you for making my day very much better." This made Haden see the humour of his mishap, but also her dilemma.

"As we are, sorry were, neighbours – you would be very welcome to stay with me till you find a new form. I could help find you one if you like. What is your name?"

"My name is Heather, and I know you because my dad used to talk about a prize fighter called Haden. With the fantastic body you have got, you *must* be him."

So this is how it came about that Haden and Heather lived together for a long time. Haden showed Heather all the sights, took her to the fights and together they spent lots of money. Which as you know, really DOES grow on trees!!!!!

The end.

Grey The Gerbil

Grey was a beige coloured gerbil that belonged to a little girl who was a very good owner as owners go she always made shore that Grey had a clean place to live and she changed the water every day and Grey's food bowl was filled every day with the best food that she could afford. At least twice a week she put Grey into a ball to run around the huge bedroom that she had and when Grey went back into his tank there was always something new either a tube or some nice treat or a toy. The tank that Grey lived in was a nice big one with a big mesh cage that sat on the top with ladders and a hammock bed that was slung from one corner across to the other there were also several sweet smelling branches that tasted nice and were fun to run around and climb on. Tubes Grey would demolish in no time but other than the branches and tubes nothing else ever got chewed. This time Grey was pleased to find a wheel hanging in his tank and he spent hours running in the wheel.

His favourite past time was trying to escape he would spend ages digging through the sawdust and sand mix to where he could see the floor, he would then spend ages working his way around the tank trying to find a way out of course he never managed to find one but when he got to the back of the tank he would stop and sit in his little hide hole bear in mind that Grey was filling his tunnel as quickly as he went and the little girl would spend ages watching the tank to see where he was. Grey did love to play hid and seek and this was probably the reason that he did because the girl hen she found him by digging up through the saw dust mix would hold Grey and stroke him and cuddle him for hours.

One day when the girl put Grey into his ball she must have been in a rush and forgotten to do the ball up tight and as Grey bumped into the tank he felt the top move so he rolled it back a bit and then hit the tank again hard and the lid moved again so he kept hitting the tank and after only five more hits the lid popped right off which meant that he was free and could take his favourite game of hide and seek to the next level. No longer did he have to play hide and seek in the tank by letting the tunnel collapse and building a nest to spend the day hiding; now he truly was free. Where to go first that was the thing there were so many interesting smells and wonderful things that he was itching to play with and a whole lot of things that were just begging to be chewed so off Grey went to explore and he was amazed how many things there were that smelt so good but tasted so bad the thing that Grey found that he liked the best was a soft sweet smelling thing that was behind some soft metal that did not taste so good but the dark soft stuff behind was fabulous. This we know to be chocolate. After his running and exploring and nibble of chocolate Grey was ready for a nice little nap so he found a nice corner where it was nice and warm behind some boxes and made himself a nest out of some bits of chewed up paper and an old sock all nestled nice and tidy in the cup of an old bra and was asleep in no time at all.

When Grey woke up it was to the sound of the door squeaking open as the little girl came in and for a moment Grey was not shore where he was although he soon remembered and was making little clicking noses with enjoyment as the little girl was hunting the ball and tank trying to find him. Grey liked the little girl so to let her know where he was, he moved along the wall and did some of the foot thumping on a box that contained one of the round things that she used to put in a box that made everything loud and vibrate. He gave the box four quick loud thumps and as quick as he could he scurried back to his nice warm nest. From there Grey could see the little girl and was pleased that she seemed calmer knowing that he was in the room and knowing that he was okay the little girl then did something that Grey did not expect she reached into the tank and took the water bottle and the sucky holder out and stuck it to the outside of the tank she then reached in and took out his food bowl and sat that next to the bottle. Well that just about said it all she was good owner and did think well of her pets. Having done this she put on the box with the moving pictures and sat down to watch it was not long after that she got undressed and climbed up the ladder and clicked of the light. Grey wasted no time he scurried across the room and had a long drink from the bottle of water. As he turned around he saw the girl looking over the top of the ladder watching him. He scurried of and went to do some more exploring several times during the night Grey would find something that made a good noise and run around on it or do his mad thumping just to tell the girl that he was still around.

The following day Grey found the girl hunting him she moved lots of things about trying to find him but there was a lot of things in the room and he was small so she did not stand much of a chance that evening when the girl had given up Grey watched her put on the moving picture box, sit down to watch. This was when Grey carefully ran across the room climbed up the chair and sat in her lap as if to say thanks for the game and as you have given up here I am. Well the girl sat there and stroked Grey whilst she watched her program then got up and put Grey back with the water and food and Grey was happy to find a new hanging chewing toy strung from the roof of the cage that was above his tank.

So the moral to this story is do not rush something important and if you sit quiet and patient then some times the thing you are hunting will come to you

The end

Harri the Hippopotamus

Harri was a hippopotamus. Hippopotamus is really a strange name, it means river horse and she lived in a river, not just any river, but she lived in the Zambezi River in Africa. Now "Hang on," I hear you say, "Harri is a male name," and you would be right, but it can also be a short name for Harriet and that is what it is in this case. Most of the other hippos thought Harri was a little strange. The reason for this is not as easy to explain as it could be, because it was not something obvious like she had an extra head or only one eye, it was something none of the other hippos could put their finger on. It was a mix of lots of little things. I mean, Harri kept herself to herself, she still remained part of the herd but always on the fringes, never in amongst them and she had a tendency to be the first one to drift to different grazing places. (Hippos are herbivores, which means they normally eat vegetation.)

Harri was also very fond of just floating with only her nostrils and eyes poking out above the water, usually among the lily pads lining the edge of the slow-moving water. This is where she would pretend to be a frog. Not that any of the others ever knew about this, but Harri had a lot of frog friends. The only ones who knew were the little tick birds which sat on her back and got rid of all the ticks and mites that used to get under her skin. Mind you, there was very little that missed their attention! They were very small and always had their eyes peeled, looking out for trouble. Although the hippos were their friends there were lots of other things in the water which *would* eat them, from snakes to crocodiles and even some of the fish were big enough to jump out and grab them. However the little tick bird that used to clean Harri most was a nice bird and did not let on to anyone about

Harri's little dream, But she and Harri would talk. It was not even this that this story is about though; can you guess what is going to happen or should I let you into the best kept secret of the Zambezi?

Harri really wanted to be a TAP DANCER! She would practice whilst she floated under the lilies. Although she kept her head still, her feet would be moving as she did all the steps. She was very graceful when in the water, it was only when she got onto dry land that everything went to pieces. I do not know if you have ever seen a hippo, but if not then I will try and describe one for you. Imagine a barrel the size of your average family car, then add four short legs, a big head which has a very wide mouth and tiny ears, put the eyes on top as well as their nostrils – now you can kind of imagine what a hippo looks like. So as you can see, they are odd looking things and as I said, on land they move very slowly, tending to be very clumsy and ungainly. It is just as well they spend most of their time in the water and are amazing swimmers.

There was one thing their size was good for and that was for defence. Only another hippo would ever give them reason to be worried about safety. The crocodiles would not even think of attacking them as they were way too big; as for the lions and tigers: well, if the hippo was on dry land then they might think about it, but it would probably be a mistake, because their mouth is huge, they have very strong jaws and four long teeth which would do serious damage to anything that got in their way.

Harri wanted more than anything to be a tap dancer and she knew that to be any good she would have to be very light on her feet, so she was constantly mindful about what she ate, trying to keep her weight down. She was always lying in the lilies practicing her dancing and, as I said, she had lots of frog friends. They knew Harri would not hurt them, so whenever danger came near they would all swim over and hide in her mouth. Sometimes there would be fifty frogs all sat in her mouth. Unfortunately this was, as you can imagine, sometimes very tickly and Harri was very ticklish. When she had a mouthful of frogs, and they were all swimming and jumping around, as you can guess sometimes she would get the back of her nose tickled (as the mouth and nose are connected) and this would make her sneeze! You can probably guess the thing that would happen next? That is right. She would fire all the frogs across the river. Now quite often the frogs would make her sneeze on purpose, as they used to find it all good fun. The trouble with doing this was if there was still danger in the water they then had to swim all the way back for safety. This was just one reason the other hippos did not get on with Harri very well.

The frogs often laughed behind Harri's back about the silly dancing she did when the other hippos were not close, but she did not allow that to distract her because she was sure that, in time, one day she would become the greatest tap dancer. One lovely warm day she was on the bank of the river eating some long grass, thinking how nice it would be to stay in the sun for a bit, but hippos cannot stay in the sun for long as they get sunburnt really easily, which is why they roll in mud. It works like a sun cream. She was dreaming away while she was eating, not paying attention and that was her BIGGEST mistake, because you must always pay attention to what is going on around you. As she took a big bite she stopped moving because she had just come face to face with a snake, and not just any snake but one called a black mamba. The name of this snake is very misleading as the snake is not actually black, but the area around the mouth is very dark. The black mamba is one of the most dangerous snakes, they are usually as long as the average human is tall, sometimes a bit more, not so very big next to a hippo.

It was still a shock, as you can see. Well, poor Harri did the only thing she could think of. She started tap dancing right onto the snake's head and it did not stand a chance against the weight of a hippo, as they can weigh up to seven tonnes and that is like having five family cars tap dancing on you. OUCH!

Unfortunately Harri was not alone. Two other hippos were standing fairly close and looked up to see what the commotion was about. They were very shocked to see the movements she was doing. The following evening they were back at the river talking to the rest of the herd, telling them about the dancing Harri was doing and why. Before long the other hippos all wanted to see her efforts. Eventually she agreed to do a dance and at first they all laughed, but Harri did not stop. Before long she became aware the laughter had stopped and turned into clapping, they were so impressed! This is how Harri became the first tap dancing hippo. She was achieving her dream.

So the moral of this story is – if you believe in something, do not give up, keep practising and if you enjoy it then don't mind if others think it odd.

Louise the leopard

Louise was a leopard and she lived in a very hot country called Africa leopards lived in wooded areas and not on the planes which is why there spots helped to camouflage them as they tended to lie in the trees and jump down on to there pray as they were a fairly small cat well by that I mean that they are a lot smaller than the lion and tiger but a little bigger than the cheetah as they have to run after there food so they stay thin but a leopard can lie in wait and pounce on its pray from above so its weight can and dose help in bringing down larger pray.

Louise did however have one little problem she was scared of heights so she would only go up on the very low branches so she tended to eat mostly little rodents like mice and rats if she was lucky then there might be the occasional small antelope that was not paying attention or a young one that had strayed from its hiding place. This being so and the fact that leopards live on there own and not as a group Louise was nearly always hungry but as she had been like it far as long as she can remember she did not mind it to much she remembers a time when she was a young leopard when she had been chasing this tree frog and as she was young she had not been listening to her mummy, her mummy had always said that she must not climb on branches that were smaller than her own wrist but she was young and was shore that she knew best but as the tree frog had hoped on to the smaller branches Louise had carried on chasing and it was not until the branch snapped that she remembered her mummy's teachings but by then it was to late. Louise tried to jump on to another branch but there were none that were big enough and she fell as she fell she hit lots of branches. Every time she hit one she got turned around so by the time she was about to get to the end of her fall she could not tell which way to twist to get her feet underneath her so when she hit the bottom she landed on her back luckily she was above the river so she hit water.

Even that was a solid landing as she had fallen a long way down and all the branches had taken there toll as she was very sore all over when Louise got her four feet back to dry land she found that she could hardly walk as the pain to her back leg was worse than she had ever felt before. It was quite a few days before she could climb and by then she was very week with hunger and also scared of falling if she had not hurt her self quite so much then she could have climbed right back up the tree.

Then she would have been fine and might not have been so scared but after a few days the fear had set in and she had never been able to cure her self of it but if she had known then she would still climb up and cure her self of it but animals do not have the sense for things like that.

Now since her mum had moved on she was on her own and there no one to help her get over these fears but she carried on as there was no other way and she had to eat. The problem was that rabbits and the like did not give her very much nutrition and there for it took her a lot longer to get better than it would if she had a partner who could hunt and get some thing better like antelope, or even better, a wild boar as they would not only fill her up but things like liver and kidneys which are filled with the good things that would help her get better are much bigger and there for she would get better quicker.

Louise's leg was a lot better and she hardly ever limped now, but the height was still a big problem and she did always remember her mum's teachings and she stayed on branches that were much bigger than her wrist and as time was passing her fear of the higher branches was growing less. On this particular day she had decided to go further north to a different part of the wooded area. Where she found a nice large tree just out of the wood there were foot prints around from antelope so she new that there were or at least were in the last few days antelope about so she decided that this would be a good place to hold up for a day or two. As she inched her way up the tree to a big branch about ten feet up she started to feel the normal fear creeping in to her hart. So having got to the branch she lay down and gently shook.

Whilst she was there she realised she could smell another leopard she froze and looked around hardly moving her head it was then that she noticed that on a branch about twice the height that she was there was another leopard and that one was bigger than her and was asleep well she felt better knowing that she had not been seen but was now not shore if she should sneak down and disappear or if she should stay and hope that he did not see her. Louise was shore from the smell and size that it was a male and about her age. As the wind was blowing from him to her then there was a if she stayed still there was a chance that he might not even see her because of her camouflage but weather there was a shift in the wind or some noise or maybe it was just that she was looking at him and he sensed it he awoke and as he moved his head he caught sight of her and stopped to get a good look.

Louise was not shore what to do she guessed that she should go but as she looked in to his eyes she could not move it was as though she had been caught in tree sap and was stuck to the branch he did one thing that nearly made her fall he smiled and gave a small grunt of hello and is was the shock that made her nearly fall as it was the last thing that she was expecting she did her best to act as though she had not been rocked to her very paws but was not shore if it had worked.

He did one more thing that was a little scary he stood up and took a good look at where she was gave another grunt of hello and flashed his eyes and held him self still then jumped landing between the trunk of the tree and her. There he stood still and then slowly he lay down. Well thought Louise as he has come down the least that I can do is to go over and say hi. So slowly Louise inched along the branch until she was the length of her tail away.

There she stopped and purred a hello and said that her name was Louise and apologised if she had done wrong by climbing in to his tree but she was looking for a new tree to hunt from and this one did look like it would be a good one. She should have guessed that it would be taken.

It is taken said the other leopard but my name is Leo and from the look of you, you need to be in a good tree for awhile and it looked from the way that you moved that you aren't very happy to be up here anyway. Well you are right I do have a little problem with height so I can only get the smaller animals so I was hoping as this is a bigger tree that it would be different but nothing has changed. Well as far as I am concerned you are welcome to stay and use this tree. To quite honest it would be nice to have some company other than the birds. Thank you that is most kind, it would be nice to be around another leopard and from the way you jumped it is obvious that you are not scared of being in the tree. Can I ask why you are? Well when I was younger I was chasing a tree frog and he went on to a branch that was too small for me to be on and it broke and I crashed to the floor hurting my leg on the way down. It was a long time till I was okay to climb and by then I was very afraid of falling.

Ahh well do you agree that I am bigger and heavier than you? Well yes of course I would be a fool to think different ok so if I go on a branch then come off then it would also take you, yes?

Well yes I guess but I am not shore it will work and besides why would you want to help me? It is a very important thing to me that you are able to provide for our kittens and you can only do that if you are okay with heights. What kittens? Are you mad? Louise said. Well only about you said Leo and I am serious, I want you to live with me I knew the moment that I woke up that you were the one for me. So how about we go for a little climb you up for it? As Louise was still in shock she just nodded and followed Leo as he jumped from branch to branch going slowly higher and higher till he stopped and turned and jumped down to where she was.

You see all you needed was a big shock and to have some thing to take your mind off your fear and you are fine so follow me down again and we can talk about what to do next.

The whole way down Louise was amazed as to how high she had gone and was bounding down as though she had been doing it all her life. When she got down to where she had been before she saw that Leo was smiling well he said you are fine now so you can stay and we can share this tree as friends if you wish or more we will see how things go. To this day there are leopards in that tree and the same family have been in that tree since Louise and Leo.

The end

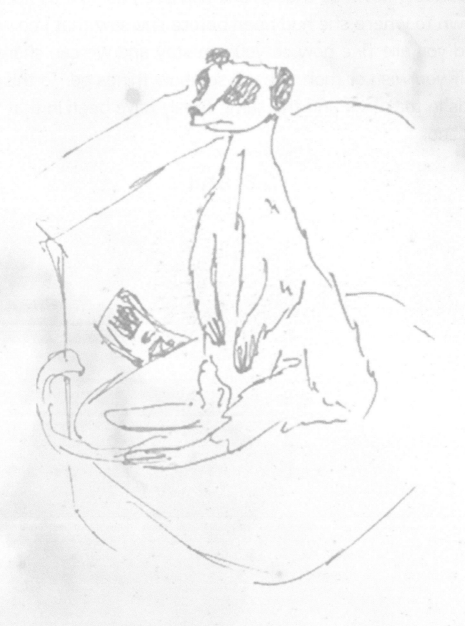

Matthew the Meerkat

Matthew was the leader of a pack of meerkats. They ran and roamed over a large area which was not too barren but nice and flat, with only a few shrubs - providing just enough shade from the hot sun which always shone upon this part of the land. They offered a good place to climb and watch for danger but they were not large enough to offer concealment to any other bands of meerkats that came passing by. Matthew's band was well off as bands go. There were fifteen couples and Matthew, being the leader, had five females under his protection. Also there were ten females who acted as floating baby-sitters. The food was plentiful, even if they did have to sometimes travel a fair way to find it.

On this particular day Matthew was leading a party of the older females over to the termite mounds found in the northern part of the area where they roamed. Now the termite offered a very high protein meal which is good, but you had to eat a lot of them to fill you up and you could not take them back to feed the others. Being filled with protein the person eating them also got filled with protein and if that person was a feeding mum, then it was very good news because that gave the milk extra nutrition, which made the babies grow big and strong. Having eaten their fill they then had to hunt for food to take back to the others. Today they were lucky as they found a large slow-worm and three scorpions, these would feed the baby-sitters very nicely.

They were returning when Matthew stopped and sat up on his hind legs, steadying himself with his tail as he searched. "For what was he searching?" I hear you ask. Well, they were returning a different way and Matthew could smell another meerkat. He knew that normally meerkats did not run around on their own so he was searching for any more, but he could only smell the one. He went on slowly and carefully. As he got closer he knew this was a female, she was from a band of meerkats living at the base of the hills way over to the north. For a long time none of this band had come onto Matthew's territory, because ages ago they had drawn up a truce as both sides had lost a lot of members due to the fighting. So to find only one and a female one at that, meant something was *very* wrong. While Matthew approached an old ground squirrel's burrow, the smell of the other meerkat became stronger, mixed with it was the smell of blood and of kittens.

Matthew took Mary, the oldest of the females he had with him, leaving all the others on watch. The two crawled down through a maze of tunnels. As they came closer to the other meerkat's hiding place they could hear its breathing – it was not sounding too good. It was sounding slow and raspy. Mary was in front and was first to find the mum and kittens. The mum was in a bad way: she was scratched up and had a bite on her shoulder. She had been there for quite some time and had no milk left, so the kittens were screaming for food. Mary helped by nursing them and let them suckle for a while. It was then the mum moved and tried to get up, but Matthew gently put a paw on her good shoulder and told her that her kittens were safe and she should save her strength for them. He went out and got one of the scorpions, dragging it down to the mum. The food, once eaten, gave the mum new strength. Matthew asked her if she was up to telling him what had happened and why was she here and alone. All she managed was, "We were attacked and I think I am the only one left." As soon as she had spoken she passed out again, but her breathing was a lot smoother.

Matthew and Mary talked it through and sort of decided it might be a good idea to leave someone here to keep an eye on them. So it was to be that Mary and Miranda, (one of the baby-sitters), stayed to look after them, keeping the kits off their mum, so she could get her strength back. Matthew would take the rest of his party back and return tomorrow with food and relief.

When Matthew got home there was the usual routine of rubbing and grooming, which always happens upon the return of a hunting party. Everyone was curious as to where Mary and Miranda were and what the strange smell was. Matthew called to the elders, whom he turned to whenever he needed help to make a decision. He told them what he knew, what he suspected to have happened, and then asked them if they thought the same, or was there something he was missing? After some time he got the response he was after: they agreed with him and if she was the only one left, then as the band she had come from was a good, loyal one, the general comment was, "Look at the way our bands talked and came to an understanding about the boundary, the way they stuck to it. This being so, then we think we should bring them into our band until they are well enough to think about what they want. If they are not the only survivors then we will nurse them till they are well, take word to Marcus' band and they can come and get them." So this was agreed.

The next morning there was a lot of activity as two of the baby-sitter meerkats and three of the young males were to go with Matthew and the hunting party. It left the band back at home a little light, but there was no danger at the moment, so it should not matter as they were not expecting to be away for very long.

Matthew and his roaming band caught some food for the hurt meerkat, Miranda and Mary. As they approached the burrow they could see Mary standing up keeping watch from the top of the pile of earth that is always found outside such holes. She was relieved to see them. "Matthew, she is much better and she is talking. You had better come down and speak to her."

Matthew took one of the baby-sitters and a snake with him and introduced himself to the stranger. Between eating and nursing, the stranger said her name was Melanie and she and her kits had escaped from her previous burrow when a roving band came and wiped out her band. "We were no match for their strength and their violence. For two days I hid and watched as the remainder were hunted and wiped out. Then I knew my only chance was to come to you. From the way Marcus talked about you I knew you were good and if I and my kits were to have any chance, it was with you and your band. This is as far as I could get. I was hurt and the going is hard, especially so with two kits in tow. Marcus was right about you. You did not kill us immediately, the way most would have done."

"OK Melanie, when you are well enough, then you can come and stay with us. I remember Marcus well, he was a good, strong leader and had he lived I know he would have thoroughly taught your kits all he could. You were a nice group to have as neighbours. What have you named your kits?" Melanie replied, "At the moment they are Millie and Marcus. He never got to see them as they were born right here in this burrow." Matthew said, "The little ones will, I am sure, grow up to be a credit to him. If you choose to stay with us, then I give you and them my promise they will know as much as possible about their father and the great leader he was. The elder's council talked and it was agreed you and they would be welcome. For now you can stay with me and I will treat them as my own. But as and when you choose to find another, then you will be free to do so. How does that sound?" Melanie was in tears. "Marcus was right about you," she stated. "He said that if anything ever happened to him I was to come straight to you, as you were one of the best. It is true, I will accept with thanks." Matthew and the band left her and went home.

It was nearly two weeks later when Melanie and the kits arrived together with the baby-sitters and the watchers. To start with Melanie was a little worried as to how everyone would react to their arrival, but true to the word of Matthew, everyone seemed pleased to see them. The kits were immediately taken off to play hide and pounce with the rest of the young ones, so Melanie and the elders could groom and rub and do the other relaxing things they needed to do in order to bond.

Later that day when Matthew returned from a foraging expedition, he was pleasantly surprised to find introductions had already been done. The meerkat pile started all over again as it was not only a welcome home to the hunters, but a full-on welcome to the band for Melanie. Millie and Marcus grew up knowing the story of their dad and the way they had arrived in this band's home. All the other baby meerkats were also taught the story, as it was believed this would make a more harmonious group. Marcus grew up treating Matthew as a dad and in time everyone thought it natural he should become second in command. Melanie proved to be a willing member of the band and stayed with Matthew; everyone could understand why Matthew had chosen her as his mate.

The end.

stephen the stallion

Stephen was a stallion, which is the name for a male horse, he lived on the plains of America right next to the Grand Canyon. As bands of horses go, the band that followed and ran with Stephen was not huge but it had been picked by him for strength and brains, not just for beauty. All of these horses were of superb quality. The Indians around there were very interested in catching them, especially Stephen, as he was very fast and the best looking stallion on the plains. Stephen was pale brown with a blond mane and tail, he also had blond eyelashes which was very unusual, as most horses have black, no matter what colour the hair on their coat.

Stephen and his band of followers knew the canyons like they knew their own smell, so never were the Indians able to trap them in a box canyon. There was something about a trap that made Stephen shiver and he would immediately turn his band of horses around and they would all escape. Only once did he get them close to being caught, but that was a few years ago. Then Stephen managed to creep into the cowboy's camp, grabbed hold of a rope holding Mary and gave it a pull with his teeth. The knot undid and they were off and running. Once clear of the camp he carefully took hold of the rope halter going around Mary's neck and pulled it over her head. Stephen was that sort of leader, which was why all the mares stayed with him. Their troubles were his and he did his best to look after all of them.

On this particular day though there was something strange on the wind. It had Stephen bothered as he could not work it out, and this made him worried. He decided to head off with his band. Keeping the wind to the side of his face he went away from the smell, after some time he changed direction and headed into the wind so whatever it was would be behind them. This way they would be safe. After a little while he caught the smell again but stronger and that was when he recognised it as being a mix of lavender, sage, brushwood, soap and horses. He remembered it from a long time ago. It brought back memories and they were pleasant ones, of a time when he was still with his mum, before the Indians had come and taken them both. He was a colt then (a colt is a very young horse) but Stephen had still managed to outrun them as soon as a chance had come his way. He still remembered the lady carer of his mum, Lilly was her name.

He recalled how well Lilly had treated them both, but Lilly was also a human and for so long humans had been something he did not trust. Then again, the cuddles and brushing she had given them were something he wished he could still have. The affectionate memory won over the fear of humans and he started walking upwind along the dry watercourse towards the smell. As he walked, more memories were starting to come back: of the good food and particularly of the black, sweet, sticky stuff she used to pour over the corn (we know the black liquid to be molasses which looks very similar to marmite and something most animals love.) Now Stephen could smell wood-smoke, bacon and coffee so he knew he was close. He told the rest of the horses to wait in the dry watercourse and be ready to run if he shouted. He slowly and carefully continued on his own and found Lilly sat next to the fire. Her horse was picketed (which means it was on a rope held to the floor with a peg) on a nice grassy area, sheltered from the wind by a large sage bush. Stephen could now smell the molasses. He went around Lilly and the fire and approaching her horse, he spent some time doing the silent talking that horses do.

Stephen was taken by surprise when he felt a brush go firmly down his side but was immediately put at ease by the gentle humming Lilly was doing. It was a song he remembered from his childhood, it was *amazing* how good it felt. "I can't remember ever feeling this good" he thought. He realised it must be six summers since he had felt a touch from a human and it felt right. Maybe it was because the lady felt good at heart, her kindness shining through. Stephen gave her a gentle nudge with his velvety nose, looked her straight in the eye and slowly walked away. He watched Lilly give her horse a stroke, walk back to the fire and climb into her bed-roll. She was undoubtedly thinking about her ranch and how good it would be to have a stallion like him there.

Stephen got back to his band of horses and gathering the lead horses together they talked about what he had found. How he thought it would be a good thing to go with Lilly.

Can you imagine Lilly's surprise when she awoke in the morning to see not one horse but a group of forty grazing! When she stood up all the horses raised their heads and looked at her, then at Stephen. Stephen shook his long, flowing mane and walking towards Lilly he nudged her gently again with his nose, she was *dumbstruck*. She made a quick breakfast and packed up camp. Mounting her horse she was pleasantly amazed when all the horses followed her. For three days Stephen and his band followed Lilly who always stopped where there was plenty of grass and good fresh water. On the fourth day she opened a gate, rode onto the flats where the grass was lush and rich and on they went until they came to some low buildings. At a lovely log cabin she dismounted, leading her horse into a nearby stable, where she gave it a rub down. Filling the corn bin she put a little molasses on it and walked away shutting the door. That was how Stephen became part of the biggest and best horse ranches in America.

The end.

Victoria the Vixen

Victoria was a female fox and lady foxes are called vixens. Victoria was an urban fox which meant she lived in town, this was good in some ways and not so good in others. It was good because there was a plentiful supply of food which could be scrounged from the bins and pavement, after all the people had gone home. It was bad because there were a lot of people. This in turn meant there were also lots of cars and dogs, these were all bad news for Victoria.

She lived in a big patch of bramble on the side of a hill overlooking the main town. It was a lovely spot to live as far as Victoria was concerned, as she had sun all day and no humans ever came close – because of the brambles. There were a few rabbits but they did not appeal, as they were very hard work in comparison with the easy pickings from the pavements and bins behind the fast food places in the high street, and from the school which was at the top of the field. All of which were devoid of people but full of food, so Victoria tended to be largely nocturnal, meaning she came out at night, although she did tend to come out in the late afternoon and spend a few lovely hours relaxing and washing in the sun. Then once the sun had gone down she would go to town or the school and start foraging for food. Her favourite pastime was .... can you guess? Chasing cats. Victoria knew lots of short cuts through holes in fences, over walls and roofs to get about unseen. She always kept both eyes and ears open on the off chance she came across a dog out late, or a human stood in the shadows, both of which could be really bad for her.

In the two summers Victoria had been living in the bramble patch only once had she had a close call. That was when a dog had come into the bramble patch. The dog was only little and was no match for her strength or ferocity. It had never returned nor was it likely to after the bites she had given it. No, she was the best and the only fox in this area. However, she had caught the scent of another fox two nights ago and since then she had not left her den, but hunger was a good persuader and she was *very* hungry. "I will just pop to the bins by the Chinese," she thought, because he was up on the hill by the school - of this she was certain. Why he was around she did not know, but she guessed it might be something to do with her being in season, but eat she must.

On her way to the Chinese Victoria used every bit of cover she could and did not stay in the open for very long. When she reached the Chinese she gave the bin a good rattle jump and off popped the lid. (A rattle jump is to run, jump all four feet against the side of the bin, pushing in the side so the air pops off the lid.) She was quietly enjoying the spicy ribs and noodles she found there, when she was startled by a voice asking "Is there enough for two?" Victoria replied "Help yourself," and backed off to go to the kebab shop four doors down. Again she gave the bin a rattle jump and was enjoying leftovers, when again came the same voice. Only this time he said "Hi! I am Frank and can I please share your bin dinner? I do not like eating alone and I definitely do not want to push you away from yours." "Well, you can if you want to" she agreed. After they had both eaten, Frank said "Thank you for dinner" and bid Victoria good night, slipping off into the shadows.

"My goodness," thought Victoria "that was not quite what I expected to happen." She wondered about him all the way back to her bramble patch. She was still thinking about him when she eventually fell asleep, just as the summer's sun was poking its nose over the rim of the horizon. When she awoke the sun was high in the sky and she ventured out to wash, sitting in the sun. Whilst she was washing her mind returned to the previous evening and Frank. She still could not work out why he had backed away.

Later, as the sun set, she again went down to the town, via the allotments to see if the chickens had been locked away. Unfortunately they were safely shut up and as she was wandering up the high street she saw Frank eating from a box on the floor. When he saw her he looked up and said "Hi, care to share?" Well, she did, and once they had finished he commented how good the sun had looked shining off her back. He also asked if she had ever eaten at the butchers. "No," she replied "where is that?" All Frank did was nod his head and walk away. Victoria was curious so she followed and after four or five doors he disappeared under a gate, around the back of a building and into a big bin on wheels that moved. Victoria followed and was amazed at the bountiful supply of food they found.

"Wow!" said Victoria, "In the two years I have been here I have not known about this place, it is a proper feast." "Well," smiled Frank "it is only right that a princess should eat at a banquet." Victoria flushed. "Where are you living anyway?" she enquired. "During the day I just hide out under a shed or in a big thorny bush," he replied. "I have a nice snug den really well hidden under a big bramble patch. You are welcome to share it if you would like to," she offered. "That would be lovely. I do not remember the last time I slept in the ground. It would be good to be back in the warm, safe ground all cosy and dry." "So it is settled then, you come home with me."

Victoria led the way and showed Frank the way to go using the most cover to get into the bottom entrance. When they were inside Frank declared, "It is no surprise you have never been found if you are always this careful when you come and go." "You are right, it is well hidden and that is only part of the reason I have never been discovered. The other is I have five entrances to my den and there is a whole maze of tunnels through the brambles. I never use the same one twice in one day, so even if I was seen it would look like I was hunting."

After many months of living together she fell pregnant and in the spring they had three more mouths to feed. That meant they had their work cut out for a while, what with foraging and all the feeding. Frank did most of the foraging and Victoria did most of the nursing. The playing was shared between them both, they found it to be a full-time job and were really tired. They were finding it hard trying to remember which entrance they used last. With all the extra coming and going plus the cubs getting more adventurous, keeping control was getting harder. All the cubs grew into fit, healthy young foxes and as they grew they found their favourite pastime was chasing pigeons, which was good stalking practice. As the summer passed, the young foxes learnt the importance of living life under cover, and all was well in the Victoria and Frank household. By the winter's end the cubs had learnt all they could from their parents, so they moved out to find their own places to set up home, only to meet up now and again as they searched for food.

The end.

Printed in the United States
By Bookmasters